RIP VAN WINKLE

Washington Irving's

RIP VAN WINKLE

ADAPTED AND WITH PAINTINGS BY

THOMAS LOCKER

Dial Books NEW YORK

Anyone who has made a voyage up the Hudson River will never forget how the Catskill Mountains rise up suddenly in the west, dwarfing the surrounding countryside. Long ago at the foot of these awesome mountains, there was a Dutch settlement in which lived a simple, good-natured, rather lazy fellow named Rip Van Winkle. Except for his wife, everyone liked Rip, especially the town's children. Sometimes he would spend the entire day playing with them. He taught them how to fly kites and told them stories about the ghosts of the mountaintops who were known to play terrible tricks on any mortal who dared to trespass on their land.

Rip was a happy-go-lucky fellow who enjoyed helping other people. He would gladly run errands for the women of the village, and if there was a stone wall to be built, his neighbors could always count on him to lend a helping hand. But taking care of his own farm was a different matter. His fields were full of weeds and stones. The roof of his house leaked, and his children were dressed in cast-off clothes. Morning, noon, and evening, Dame Van Winkle would scold Rip about the ruin he was bringing upon his family with his idleness. Rip's only reply to these tirades was to shrug his shoulders and sneak away.

One fine day, with coins jingling in his pocket from selling off the last few acres of his family's land, Rip arrived at the village inn. He spent a long afternoon with his friends and was soon feeling mellow. But the tranquility of the day was suddenly shattered. The furious Dame Van Winkle burst in, screaming at the top of her lungs. She yelled at Rip for selling the land and then turned her wrath upon his friends, accusing them of encouraging Rip's bad habits. From that day on she hunted him down all over the village, and there was nowhere for him to hide.

Poor Rip! Now the only way he could escape the labor of the farm and the clamor of his wife was to take his gun and go hunting deep in the woods. One crisp autumn day Rip and his faithful dog, Wolf, scrambled up one of the tallest mountains in search of squirrels. Tired from the day's hunt, Rip lay down on a grassy knoll. All at once he heard a voice calling from the glen: "Rip Van Winkle! Rip Van Winkle!" The hair on Wolf's back bristled. Rip was startled, but guessing that one of his neighbors needed assistance, he hurried to help.

As Rip approached the spot where the voice seemed to have come from, he saw a short, squarely built old man dressed in the ancient Dutch style. The man was carrying a stout keg, and without uttering a word he motioned to Rip to take it. Then the stranger turned and led him farther up into the mountains. The old man was totally silent, and Rip grew frightened. As he struggled under his heavy burden, he heard a sound like rolling thunder in the distance.

Trembling with fear, Rip obeyed. Even though they appeared to be having a celebration, Rip had never beheld a more mournful group of men. The Dutchmen drank in profound silence and returned to their game. Rip was unnerved, but when no one was looking, he decided to try their brew himself. He found that he liked it, and one taste led to another, and another. His head began to swim and the world started to fade. As the last rose-colored light left the sky Rip Van Winkle fell into a deep sleep.

Awakened by the bright morning sunlight, Rip opened his eyes. Where am I? he wondered. Isn't this the place where I first saw the Dutchman? How did I get here? Did I sleep here all night? He remembered the strange night and the strong drink. How will I ever explain this to my wife? he thought. As he got up to look for his dog and his gun, he found himself stiff in his joints. He was astonished to discover that he was dressed in rags, and instead of his well-oiled gun he found a rusty, worm-eaten flintlock lying nearby. "Those Dutchmen — they robbed me!" he cried.

Rip was angry, and he determined to go back to the hollow and demand that they return his things. Painfully he retraced his steps until he reached the entrance to the hollow. To his amazement no trace of the opening remained. The ravine had become a high wall with a waterfall tumbling down into a dark pool. Rip tried to scale the wall, but found that it was impossible. He whistled for his dog, but only the cawing of a flock of idle crows mocked his call. Poor Rip realized that he was famished, and he grieved for the loss of his dog and gun. He shook his head, shouldered the rusty flintlock, and turned his steps homeward.

As he entered his village Rip thought, What in the world is going on? Who are all these strangers, and what are these new buildings doing here? There weren't any when I set out yesterday! The people seemed equally surprised at the sight of Rip. Whenever they looked at him, they stroked their chins, and without thinking Rip repeated their gesture. He felt something on his chin, and glanced down at himself. He was astonished to discover that he had grown a long white beard. I've been bewitched! he thought.

Rip almost got lost trying to find his own house. Everything had changed! He was so bewildered that he almost longed to hear the shrill voice of his wife, but when he finally found his house, it was empty and fallen to ruin. Rip called out, but the rooms only echoed the sound of his voice. Then all was silent. "Oh," he sobbed, "what has happened to me?" Stumbling out he ran toward the inn, praying that he would find a friend. But when he arrived, there was only a crowd of strangers listening to a politician near a strange red, white, and blue flag.

Rip's wild appearance and frantic questions attracted the attention of the crowd. A pretty young woman with a child pressed forward to get a better look. The child was frightened by Rip's appearance and began to cry. "Hush, Rip, that old man won't hurt you," assured the mother. The child's name, and something familiar about the mother's looks, made Rip blurt out, "Young woman, what is your father's name?"

"Ah, poor man!" she replied. "He was named Rip Van Winkle, but it is twenty years since he went off hunting and never returned."

"And your mother?" gasped Rip.

"Oh, she collapsed and died a few years ago while yelling at a Yankee peddler."

Rip couldn't contain himself any longer. He caught his daughter in his arms saying, "Judith! I'm your father. Oh, doesn't anyone remember me?"

At first the crowd thought Rip must be crazy. Then the oldest man in the village came closer and peered at Rip. "I remember you, Rip Van Winkle. Welcome home, old neighbor. Why, where have you been these twenty long years?" When Rip told his story, many in the crowd shook their heads in disbelief. The old fellow, however, said, "I believe Rip is telling the truth. It's well known that the ghosts of Henry Hudson and his crew return every twenty years to the river and the mountains they discovered so long ago. My own father once saw the Dutchmen playing at ninepins in a hollow in the mountains."

To make a long story short, Rip's daughter took him home to live with her family. Having reached the age when a man can be idle without reproach, Rip spent the rest of his days either down in the village telling travelers his story, or up on the hill teaching children how to fly kites in the wind over the river. And to this day, whenever inhabitants of Rip's village hear the distant roll of thunder coming from the mountains, they say, "That must be old Henry Hudson playing at ninepins again!"

For Kellie Campbell

Published by Dial Books
A Division of NAL Penguin Inc.
2 Park Avenue
New York, New York 10016

Published simultaneously in Canada
by Fitzhenry & Whiteside Limited, Toronto
Copyright © 1988 by Thomas Locker
Printed in U.S.A.
First Edition
(a)
1 3 5 7 9 10 8 6 4 2

Library of Congress Cataloging in Publication Data

Locker, Thomas, 1937—
Rip Van Winkle.

Summary: A man who sleeps for twenty years in the
Catskill Mountains awakens to a much-changed world.
[1. Catskill Mountains Region (N.Y.)—Fiction.
2. New York (State)—Fiction.] I. Irving, Washington,
1783–1859. Rip Van Winkle. II. Title.
PZ7.L7945Ri   1988   [Fic]   87-24448
ISBN 0-8037-0520-4
ISBN 0-8037-0521-2 (lib. bdg.)

The art for each picture consists of an oil painting
that is color-separated and reproduced in full color.